HOW TO BE AN OLDER BROTHER OR SISTER

(WHAT TO EXPECT WHEN IT HAPPENS TO YOU)

WRITTEN AND ILLUSTRATED BY MIKE VENEZIA

 CHILDRENS PRESS ®

CHICAGO

To Jeannine, Mike, Liz, Tony, and Debbie

Library of Congress Cataloging-in-Publication Data

Venezia, Mike.
    How to be an older brother or sister.

    (Easy reading picture stories)
    Summary: An older sibling experiences the ups and
downs of having a new baby in the family and sharing
the years of growth that follow.
    [1.   Brothers and sisters—Fiction.   2.   Babies—
Fiction]   I.   Title.   II.   Series.
PZ7.V557Ho   1986   [E]   85-27977
ISBN 0-516-03494-4

This isn't going to be easy.

Things will be different.
First you have to get used
to all the people.

Sometimes it's hard to
get some sleep.

You worry. You never know
when it could happen again.

Most of the time you can't even
make a little bit of noise.

Learning to share things
starts early.

Your mom might let you
help feed them if you're
careful. That's fun.

When they start eating big
people food that's *really* fun.

You can expect to sit around a lot
while people take pictures.

You can't even get mad
at them 'cause they don't
know what they're doing.

And nothing is safe.

You have to protect them sometimes.

When they start to walk
anything can happen.

And when they get older
things can get worse.

Sometimes they throw
stuff in the toilet.

Because you're bigger
you always get blamed.

They can walk in on
you at any time.

They can ask the worst
questions at the worst times.

But try to remember
there is always someone
worse off than you.

Sometimes it's good to
have them around, like when
they make stuff just for you.

When none of your
friends are around, you
can play with them.

You can read them
your favorite stories.

And its fun to teach them
new things, like how to swim,

or paint,

or ride a bike,

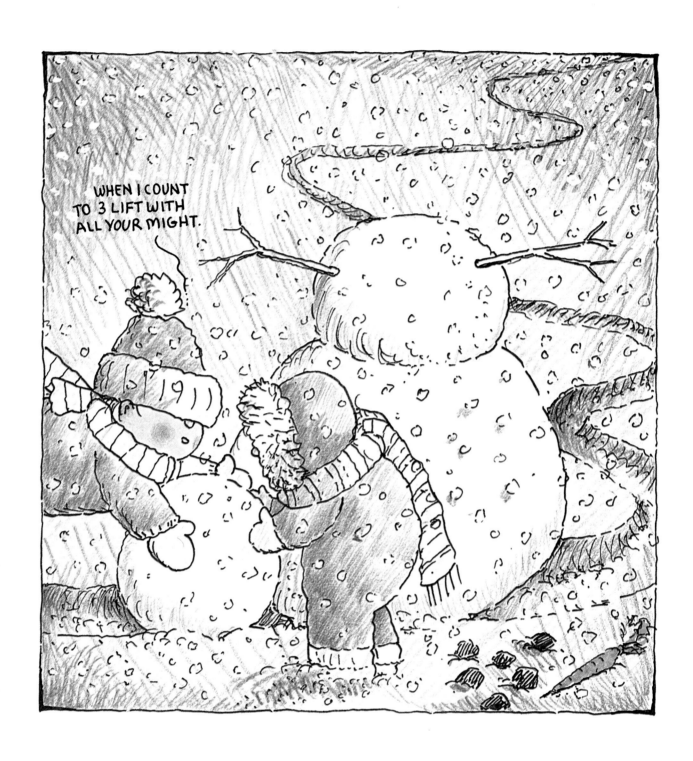

or build a snowman.

You can help them
learn games.

When there's thunder they
might come into your bed.

So it's really not so bad.
But just when you
think you've got a
handle on it. . .